Weekly Reader Children's Book Club presents

Stories from a Snowy Meadow

Stories from Snowy Meadow

by Carla Stevens
pictures by Eve Rice

A Clarion Book
The Seabury Press ❋ New York

For Marie and Mac

The Seabury Press, 815 Second Avenue, New York, N.Y. 10017

Text copyright © 1976 by Carla Stevens
Illustrations copyright © 1976 by Eve Rice
Designed by Victoria Gomez
Printed in the United States of America

Library of Congress Cataloging in Publication Data
Stevens, Carla.   Stories from a snowy meadow.
"A Clarion book."
Summary: Mole, Mouse, and Shrew love to visit Old
Vole and listen to her stories. Then one day she dies,
and her friends compose a song of tribute to her.
[1. Friendship—Fiction. 2. Death—Fiction]
I. Rice, Eve. II. Title.
PZ7.S8435St   [Fic]   76-3542   ISBN 0-8164-3161-2

Contents

1 ❊ The Quilt

Icy winds blew across fields and woods.

It was snowing.

But Mole and Shrew and Mouse were not cold. Below the ground, in Mole's burrow home, they were sitting near the fireplace sewing patches for a quilt.

"What shall we do with the quilt when we finish it?" Mouse asked.

"We should have thought of that before we started," Shrew said.

Mouse sighed. "I never thought it was going to be so beautiful."

"It is a cold winter," Shrew said. "I need a quilt to keep me warm."

"But I need it more than you do." Mouse said. "I have only one blanket to cover me."

Mole pushed his chair back and stretched his legs. "Maybe we should give it to someone."

"You mean give it away?" asked Mouse and Shrew.

"Yes," said Mole. "To someone who needs it."

"You mean, after all our hard work, we just give it away?" Mouse shook his head. "Never!"

"Certainly not!" Shrew said.

"I have a good idea," said Mouse. "Let's draw straws. The one who draws the shortest straw gets the quilt."

"That's fair," Shrew said. "But let's finish the quilt first."

"I can't sew any longer today," Mole said. "I promised to bring some leek soup to Vole."

"I haven't seen Vole in a long time. How is she?" asked Shrew.

"Why don't you come with me and see for yourself?"

"I want to come too," Mouse said.

Mole and Shrew and Mouse bundled up. They set off for Vole's house. Mole carried the soup.

It was cold outside. The snow was falling very fast. It covered their tracks soon after they passed by.

When they reached Vole's house, Mole said, "Don't knock."

"Why not?" asked Shrew.

"She's in bed and cannot get up."

"What's the matter with her?" Mouse asked.

"She's very old," Mole said.

"Oh," said Mouse. "Is that all?" And he opened the door.

"Hello there, Vole," called Mole.

"Come in, come in," said a small, weak voice. Vole was sitting up in bed. She had a shawl over her shoulders.

"I brought you some soup."

"Thank you, Mole," said Vole.

"It's freezing in here," whispered Shrew. "The fire is out in her stove."

"There is some wood outside her door," Mouse said.

Mouse and Shrew filled the stove with wood. They lighted the fire. Soon the room was warm.

Mole heated the soup and gave some to
Vole.

"Mmmm!" she said. "This good soup reminds me of a story. Would you like to hear
it?"

"Yes, yes," said Mouse and Shrew and
Mole. And they moved closer to her bed to
listen.

*O*nce upon a time, there was an old, old vole.

"Is this a story about you?" asked Mouse.
"Perhaps," answered Vole. "Listen."

Long ago, the old vole's children had grown up and moved away. But she stayed in the little home where she had lived all her life.

One very cold night, she heard a knock on her door. She opened it.

In the doorway stood a large cricket. "Please let me in," said the cricket, shivering. "I'm freezing."

The old vole opened her door wide. The cricket hopped over to the fireplace and sat down on the hearth.

"You must be hungry," said the old vole.

"Oh, I am," said the cricket.

The old vole gave the cricket a crust of bread dipped in milk.

As soon as the cricket had eaten the bread, he began to sing. First he sang "Down in the Valley" and then he sang "Skip to my Lou."

"You have a beautiful voice," said the old vole.

"Thank you," answered the cricket. "If you let me live here, I'll sing for you often."

"That would be nice," said the old vole.

"And," the cricket added, "I will also give you a present."

"Oh, you don't have to give me anything. I am lonely. Sing and keep me company."

The cricket reached into his pocket. "Here," he said. "This white pebble is my present. Put it in your soup pot. Fill the pot with water and put it over the fire to boil. When the water boils, taste it."

"Why, it's just a plain old pebble," thought the old vole. But she didn't want to hurt the cricket's feelings. She put the pebble in her soup pot and filled the pot with water.

"Now boil it," said the cricket.

The old vole felt silly boiling a pebble but she did as she was told.

After a while, the cricket said, "The water is boiling."

"So it is," said the old vole.

"Well, what are you waiting for?" the cricket asked. "Taste it."

So the old vole dipped her big spoon into the pot. She blew on the spoon to cool it. Then she tasted it. "Ah!" she said in surprise.

She took another sip. "Oh my!" Why it was

broth, not water at all, the very best broth she had ever had.

"This is delicious!" exclaimed the old vole. "How can this be? I know I only poured water into my pot."

"Never mind," said the cricket. "As long as the pebble is in the pot, you will never be hungry."

He began to sing again—"The Blue Tail Fly."

This time the old vole knew the words, so she joined in the chorus.

And that was just how Cricket and Old Vole spent many cheerful evenings together for a long, long time.

❃ ❃ ❃

"I wish I had a magic pebble like that," sighed Mouse.

"That was a good story, Vole," Shrew said. "Tomorrow, I'll bring you more wood."

"I'll stop by with some seeds," added Mouse.

"Good-by," called the three friends.

"Good-by," answered Vole.

The wind blew the snow in great swirls across the meadow. It was very hard for Mole to see, but Shrew led the way back to Mole's house.

Mouse spoke first when they were indoors once again. "I could tell from Vole's story that she is lonely. I wonder if I'm going to be lonely when I am old."

"About that quilt, Mole," said Shrew.

"What about it?"

"It would just fit Vole's bed."

"Yes, it would," said Mouse. "Do you know what I think? I think we made it for her, only we didn't know it at the time."

"If we work hard, we can finish it in time for her birthday," said Mole.

"That's a good idea!" Shrew and Mouse said.

And once again, the three friends sat down to sew beside the fire.

2 ✽ The Birthday Party

It was Friday. Mouse and Shrew spread the quilt on Mole's bed.

"There are eight stars," Mouse said. "I just counted them."

"I can't wait until Vole sees it," Shrew said.

"Be patient, Shrew," said Mole. "I've almost finished decorating the cake. There now. Are we ready?"

"You carry the quilt, Mouse," Shrew said. "You're bigger than I am."

Mole closed the door behind him. "The candles! We forgot the candles!"

"I'll get them," Shrew said. He ran back into the house.

It was a cold, clear day. A hard crust of snow covered the meadow, making travel easier.

"Let's sing happy birthday as we walk in," said Mouse.

"First I'll light the candles," Shrew said. "Ready?" He opened the door.

> *"Happy birthday to you,*
> *Happy birthday to you,*
> *Happy birthday dear Vole,*
> *Happy birthday to you."*

"Oh my!" said Vole, who was sitting up in bed. "What a surprise! I had almost forgotten today is my birthday."

"We didn't forget," said the three friends. "Make a wish!"

Vole closed her eyes for a moment. Then she opened them again. "I won't tell you my wish because then it might not come true."

She took a deep breath and blew as hard as she could. All the candles went out except one.

"Quick! Blow again!" said Mouse.

Vole sucked in her breath. She blew once more and the last candle went out.

"Hooray!" the friends shouted.

"You cut the first piece and I'll cut the rest," Mole said.

Vole took a bite of the cake. "Mmmm. It is delicious, Mole."

"Now we have a present for you," said Shrew. "Help me unfold it, Mouse."

Mouse and Shrew unfolded the quilt and spread it on Vole's bed.

"It is the most beautiful quilt I have ever seen," Vole said. "And how warm it feels. Thank you my good friends. I wish I could do something for you in return."

"You can tell us another story," Mouse said.

"Yes! Yes!" said Mole and Shrew. "Tell us a story."

Vole began.

There was once a little Shrew who lived all by herself. Once in a while she was lonely, but most of the time she was not. She read, wrote stories, drew pictures, and took walks.

One winter morning, she bundled herself up to go out for a walk. She opened her door and Whoopo! She almost fell over a big pile of shoes.

What a surprise! There was a pair of red shoes, a pair of blue shoes, a pair of sneakers, big black rubber boots, and a pair of fuzzy slippers.

Little Shrew put her foot alongside the rubber boots. She could tell they were much too big.

Next, she put her foot alongside a red shoe but it didn't fit either.

What should she do? She just couldn't leave all those shoes on her doorstep. She might fall over them going in and out.

So she carried them inside and put them in her closet. All day long she kept thinking about the shoes and wondering who could have left them.

The next morning, when she was eating her cereal, she heard a rustling at the door.

She went to the door and opened it. There on the doorstep was a large bundle.

She looked more closely. There was a red jacket, three pairs of pants, and a long muffler.

She held the pants up. Too big.

And the jacket. Much too big.

"Well, at least the muffler is the right size," she thought.

It was silly. All these clothes, and nothing she could wear except the muffler. She put them in the closet along with the rest of the things

All day long she thought about the shoes and clothes. Were they presents? If so, who was leaving them for her? And why wasn't anything the right size?

It took a long time for Little Shrew to fall asleep that night.

The next morning, she again heard a rustling at the door, and she knew someone or something was there.

And she was right.

There on her doorstep was a big bag. It had a large tag tied to the top. The tag said:

PLEASE DON'T PLAY WITH MY TOYS
UNTIL I GET THERE.

Toys! Little Shrew opened the bag and

peeked in. She could see checkers and a check-erboard, a yo-yo, a kite, two balls, crayons, and a game of Monopoly.

Little Shrew thought about the tag:

UNTIL I GET THERE.

Someone was coming.
But who?
And when?
She put the bag in her closet.

Little Shrew was so excited that she couldn't sleep all night.

First, she imagined that a dragon was coming. But no, a dragon wouldn't have three pairs of pants.

Then she thought of a bear. But of course a bear would be too big for the red jacket.

Then she thought of a worm. But worms don't wear boots.

Just as it was beginning to get light, Little Shrew tiptoed out of bed and went over to her door and listened.

No noise except the soft humming of the wind. So she sat down and waited.

Soon she heard a rustling. Then a shuffling and then sliding.

The sliding sound was getting louder and louder. Little Shrew was frightened. Should she open the door?

For a moment she thought she should not. But then she did. And there on her doorstep was a large box.

On the box was a sign. It said:

DO NOT OPEN BEFORE CHRISTMAS

But someone had crossed out DO NOT *with a red crayon.*

"Open before Christmas," thought Little Shrew. "That must mean right now."

So she very slowly and very carefully lifted the top off the box. And there looking up at her was a mole with a big red bow around his neck.

Little Shrew jumped back in surprise. "What are you doing in there?" she gasped.

DO NOT OPEN
BEFORE
CHRISTMAS

"I'm a present," said the mole. "From me to you."

"But Christmas is over, and my birthday isn't until March," said Little Shrew.

"I'm a late Christmas present and an early birthday present looking for a home," said the mole. "Where did you put my slippers?"

Little Shrew thought about her late Christmas present and early birthday present. It could talk and laugh and play checkers and Monopoly and fly a kite and even help with the dishes.

"Just what I've always wanted!" she said out loud. "Please come in. Your slippers are in the closet."

And Mole and Little Shrew lived quite happily together for a long time.

❋　❋　❋

Mouse and Shrew and Mole clapped. "That was a good story!" they said.

"I have had many, many presents," Vole said. "But this quilt is the best present I have ever had." She lay back in bed and sighed.

"Vole, you look tired. We will go now and let you rest," Mole said.

"I feel so warm and cozy under my beautiful quilt. Thank you again, dear friends."

"Happy birthday!" they called as they left Vole's house.

Outside, icicles hung from the branches and every little while one fell, tinkling like broken glass on the crusty snow.

3 ❀ Mole Is Not Mole

It was a whole week later when Mouse knocked on Mole's door.

"Go away," said a voice that did not sound like Mole.

"Mole, is that you?" Mouse asked.

"It is I," said Mole. "Go away."

Mouse opened the door a crack and peeked inside.

Mole was sitting by the fire all bundled up. "Don't bother me," he said. "You're always bothering me. Go away."

"All right," Mouse said. "I'm going." And he closed the door.

On his way home, Mouse met Shrew.

"Something is wrong with Mole. He told me
to go away."

"He did?" asked Shrew. "That doesn't sound
like Mole."

"He said, 'you're always bothering me. Go
away.' "

"That's funny," said Shrew. "I think I'll go
and see him myself."

Shrew went to Mole's house and knocked on
the door.

"What do you want?" asked a hoarse voice.

"May I come in, Mole?" asked Shrew.

"No!" said the voice. "Go away."

Shrew opened the door. "What is the matter, Mole?"

"You're bothering me. That's what is the matter."

Shrew closed the door. He went to find Mouse. "Something *is* the matter with Mole."

"I told you so," said Mouse. "Let's go to see Vole. Maybe she can tell us what's wrong."

Mouse and Shrew went to Vole's house.

Vole was knitting by the fire. "Hello, Mouse. Hello, Shrew. It is good to see you again. Did you come to hear another story?"

"Not today, Vole," said Shrew. "We have a problem."

"Goodness!" said Vole.

"This morning Mouse went to see Mole and Mole told him to go away. Then I went to see Mole and Mole said in a funny, hoarse voice, 'You're bothering me. Go away.' "

"Why, Mole reminds me of my very best friend," said Vole. "Let me tell you about something that happened a long time ago. This is a true story."

When I was young, my very best friend lived next door. Her name was Mousie.

One day Mousie and I decided to go on a picnic. I made the lunch, put it in a basket, and then went to Mousie's house.

Mousie didn't seem very glad to see me. The first thing she said was, "I always have to carry everything. This time you carry the picnic basket."

"That's funny," I thought. "I am already carrying the basket." But I didn't say anything because Mousie was my very best friend.

So we started off. We walked for a little while.

Suddenly Mousie stopped. She looked very cross. "You're walking too fast. You always walk too fast."

I began to walk very, very slowly.

Soon we reached a shady spot near a brook. "What a nice place for a picnic," I said.

Mousie looked even more cross. "You always pick the place. It's my turn to pick the place."

I said, "All right. You pick the place."

We walked a few more steps. Then Mousie said in a loud, hoarse voice, "Here."

So I put the basket down and began to unpack the lunch. I gave Mousie a sandwich.

"Ick!" she said.

"But I thought you liked peanut butter!" I said.

"Today, I HATE peanut butter," Mousie said.

"Well, how about an apple?" I asked.

"I HATE apples," Mousie said.

"I know you like chocolate cake," I said timidly.

"You don't know that at all," Mousie said. And she stamped her foot. "Today I HATE chocolate cake!"

"Apple juice?"

"NO! You didn't bring any of the right things. You NEVER bring any of the right things. I'm going home. GOOD-BY!"

And off she went.

*I sat for a while thinking about Mousie.
Then I ate a peanut butter sandwich, an apple
and two pieces of chocolate cake. I drank all
the apple juice.*

*After I ate my lunch, I made up my mind
that Mousie was not my best friend any more.
Then I went home.*

*The next morning I found a note under my
door. It said:*

Dear Vole,

> *I can't swallow.*
> *I have the mumps.*
> *You will know when you are*
> *getting them because you will*
> *feel very, very cross.*
> *Your best friend,*
> *Mousie*

> *P.S.*
> *When my mumps go away,*
> *let's have another picnic.*

❊ ❊ ❊

"Did you get the mumps?" Mouse asked.

"Oh yes," said Vole. "And then it was my turn to be cross."

"Now I understand," Shrew said. "Mole doesn't feel well. When you don't feel well, you can be very grumpy."

"You mean Mole's just sick?" asked Mouse. "Then we must do something to help him."

"Good-by, Vole. Thanks for that good story."

Shrew and Mouse went back to Mole's house. "Mole! May we come in?"

There was a loud sneeze. Then they heard, "NO!"

Mouse opened the door. "Poor Mole. You must feel terrible. Get right into bed. I will make you some camomile tea."

Mole blew his nose. "Go away," he said weakly.

"We'll go," Shrew said. "But first we have things to do."

Shrew straightened Mole's bed.

Mouse made tea from camomile leaves and gave Mole a cup.

"I ache all over," said Mole. And he sneezed again.

"Poor Mole! You will feel better when you have had a nap," said Shrew. He helped Mole climb into bed. "We'll come back later and make supper for you."

Mole pulled the covers way over his head.

Mouse and Shrew looked at the lump on the bed. They quietly closed the door.

"Do you think he has the mumps?" asked Mouse. "I've never had the mumps."

"Oh, no," said Shrew. "Mole just has a bad cold. Let's go back and tell Vole that soon Mole will be his old self again."

4 * An End
and a Beginning

Two weeks later, in early March, Mole was sweeping his kitchen when he heard Mouse calling to him.

"Mole, Mole, come quick! Something terrible has happened. Vole is dead!"

Mole opened the door. "Are you sure, Mouse?" he asked.

"Yes. I was bringing her some seeds this morning. She didn't answer when I knocked. I thought she was taking a nap. When I tiptoed over to her bed, I knew. She was cold and still."

"She must have died in her sleep," said Mole.

Mouse began to cry.

"Wait, Mouse. Let me get my jacket. We will go to see Vole together."

On the way they stopped at Shrew's house.

"Shrew!" Mole called. "Come quickly. Mouse thinks Vole is dead."

"Oh, no!" said Shrew. "I'll be right there."

"Here, take my handkerchief, Mouse," said Mole.

Mouse took Mole's handkerchief and blew his nose. "If only I had visited her more often," he sobbed.

Shrew came out pulling on his jacket. "Oh, dear," he said. "How sad."

The three friends hurried to Vole's house.

Vole lay on the bed, covered by her quilt. Mouse began to sob more loudly.

"Come, come Mouse," Mole said a little sharply. "Vole was very old. She led a full and happy life. It was time for her to die."

"If only I had talked to her one more time." Mouse blew his nose again.

"I wish I had done more for her," Shrew said.

"Yes, we all do," Mole said. "I wonder where she would want to be buried."

"Under the oak tree?" asked Mouse, thinking of his favorite place.

"She used to sun herself on the leaf pile near the stone wall," said Shrew.

"But she loved the meadow the best," said Mole. "I know a place near the brook. It will be easier to dig there. The ground is not so frozen."

"First, we must build a box to bury her in," said Shrew. "I have lots of wood at home."

They walked back to Shrew's house. Mouse boiled water for tea while Mole and Shrew made plans to build the box.

"Tea is ready," said Mouse. "But I don't want any." And his eyes filled with tears.

Mole handed Mouse a biscuit. "There. Eat this," he said. "You will feel better."

Mouse nibbled at the biscuit. "If only she had blown out all her candles."

"Don't be so silly, Mouse. That would not have made any difference," Mole said. "She was very old. When I am very old, I will die too."

Mole began sawing wood while Shrew nailed the pieces together. At last the box was built.

"It's not fancy," said Mole. "But it seems just right for Vole."

"It's a good box," Shrew said. "You take one end while I take the other."

"All right," said Mole.

"I want to help, too," Mouse said.

"You carry the shovel and open and close all the doors, Mouse."

They carried the box to Vole's house and set it down near her bed. Mole and Shrew picked her up and laid her in it.

"Let's cover her with the quilt," Mouse said.

"No," said Mole. "She would want someone to have her quilt. We must give it away to someone who will love and need it as she did." And Mole began to nail down the cover.

Mole and Shrew lifted the box again. They walked slowly across the meadow to the brook. Here and there, spears of grass showed through the soft snow.

"This is the place I was thinking of," Mole said. "In the spring, violets and trout lilies bloom here."

Mole and Shrew set the box down. Mole took the shovel from Mouse and began to dig.

After a few minutes, Shrew took a turn digging.

"I want to help, too," Mouse said, taking the shovel.

Then Mole said, "The hole is big enough now."

He and Shrew picked up the box and lowered it into the ground.

"I've been thinking of a poem," Mouse said.

"Dear Vole, wise and kind,
And very old.
I loved the stories
That you told.
And even though
You are not here,
Your words are singing
In my ears."

Mole began to shovel dirt on the box. Soon it was covered, a large brown spot surrounded by a blanket of snow.

A warm breeze blew, rustling the old oak leaves still clinging to their branches overhead.

Mole sniffed the air. "Spring is almost here," he said. "Tomorrow we'll tidy up Vole's house. Someone will be needing a new place to live soon."

"But not someone as nice as Vole," said Mouse.

Shrew picked up the shovel. "Say your poem again, Mouse."

The three friends started back across the meadow.

"Dear Vole, wise and kind,
And oh, so old.
We loved the stories
That you told.
And even though
You are not here
Your words are singing
In our ears."